GirlFriendZ

Music is
NOT
banned!

GirlFriendZ
The Day the Music Died
by Roger Hurn
Illustrated by Kenny Kiernan

Published by Ransom Publishing Ltd.
Radley House, 8 St. Cross Road, Winchester, Hampshire
SO23 9HX, UK
www.ransom.co.uk

ISBN   978 178127 150 6
First published in 2013

The Day
the Music
Died

Roger Hurn

Illustrated by Kenny Kiernan

Ransom

Kelly Montez

Like · Comment · Friend

Hey, I'm Kelly Montez, and unless you've been living in a cave for the past year you'll know I'm in the band *GirlFriendZ*.

Yeah, that's right, I'm the one with the killer looks and a voice like gravel dipped in honey. And *GirlFriendZ* is the number one band in the world – or it *was*, until the day the aliens invaded Earth and banned music! Those creepoids are *so* not cool.

But don't worry guys, we're not going to let them get away with that. *GirlFriendZ* will carry on making music and there's no way a bunch of alien weirdos in MIB (Music is Banned) is going to stop us!

Yaz Jackson

Like · Comment · Friend

Hiya guys, Yaz here. I was born in a circus and my mum and dad were acrobats, so that's why I'm always doing somersaults, cartwheels and back flips on stage. On our next tour I'm gonna walk across the stage on a high wire! How cool is that?

Yeah, you did hear me right. There WILL be another *GirlFriendZ* tour – just as soon as we find a way to send the Zargons back to their home planet with their creepy alien tails between their legs.

Olivia Parsons

Like · Comment · Friend

Hi *GirlFriendZ* fans. My name is Olivia – but everyone calls me Liv. I know I look like the girl next door, but I can be a bit of a wild child when it comes to music! I just love getting up on stage and singing my heart out!

But now those freaky aliens are arresting musicians and destroying all the musical instruments they can get their tentacles on! It makes me so mad, but they'll never catch us and stop us singing.

That's a promise!

Eve Rossi

Like · Comment · Friend

Hello everybody. I'm Eve, the girl with the crazy hair and the personality to match!

It's great being in *GirlFriendZ* 'cos it gives me the chance to wear all kinds of amazing outfits. I love designing my own clothes and it gives me a buzz when I see you guys copying my look!

I know the Zargons are trying to stop us having fun – but don't fret guys, we are *so* gonna have the last laugh!

Charlotte Opirah

Like · Comment · Friend

OK, it's me, Charlotte. Usually I'd rather sing than talk, 'cos I'm the best singer in the band. Hey, just kidding!!

But I've got something to say that can't be put into a song. It's this. We absolutely *have* to find a way to beat the Zargons! They must have a weakness – and I've got a suspicion it has something to do with music.

Think about it guys. They have banned music and they're doing some kind of alien mind-wipe, so musicians and singers forget how to play and sing. Why? Well, I'm gonna make it my business to find out!

Finn the roadie

Like · Comment · Friend

Hey, I'm Finn and I have the best job in the world. I'm the *roadie* (that's road manager) for *GirlFriendZ*. Well, it *was* the best job until the Zargons arrived and we had to go on the run. Now my job is about getting the girls to their secret gigs *and* keeping them out of the Zargon's clutches! You see, the Zargon agents of MIB track down musicians and singers and take them off to the 'harmony' camps to have their minds wiped. Then, when they come out of the camps, they can't remember how to play or sing.

GirlFriendZ are the last band left, so MIB are desperate to catch them. If they do that, then that really *will* be the day music dies. But I'm never going to let that happen!

9

The Zargons

The Zargons are an alien race from the Andromeda galaxy. They have developed advanced technology that enables their starships to travel faster than the speed of light.

They are humanoid in appearance and, contrary to popular opinion, they do not possess tentacles (or tails!). However, in certain conditions, their eyes glow like cats' eyes.

They are on a mission to eradicate all forms of music from the universe. To this end, the Zargons build 'harmony' camps on the planets they invade. Anyone with musical talent is taken to the camps by Zargon agents of MIB (*Music Is Banned*), where they are subjected to a process known as 'mind wiping'. The mind–wipe has the effect of making the musician or singer forget how to play or sing. In street slang this process is known as 'soul stealing'.

The main feature of the 'harmony' camps are the giant incinerators where musical instruments are destroyed.

It is believed that the Zargons' hatred of music stems from the fact that music is the only thing that has the power to defeat them. (See article: *vampires*, *garlic*, *crosses*.)

Prologue

London, England. Saturday 2nd August 2025

'Thank you Wembley. It's been emotional.'

Kelly punched the air with her fist and 70,000 fans screamed back at her. Yaz, Olivia, Eve and Charlotte, the other members of *GirlFriendZ*, jumped up and down on the stage like hyperactive kangaroos. Waves of love washed over them from their fans. If they hadn't known they were the world's biggest band before this gig – they knew it now!

'Hey, listen to those guys,' yelled Charlotte.

'Yay, it's awesome,' Eve yelled back at her.

Olivia grinned like a cat with a bowl of double cream. 'It just doesn't get any better than this.'

'Yes it does,' said Yaz. 'This show's being beamed worldwide by satellite. Billions of people are going mad for us.'

* * * * * * *

Suddenly a huge shadow covered the stadium. The howling crowd fell silent. A giant starship hovered over Wembley.

At first people thought it was part of the show. But then a red laser light shot out from the ship and vapourised the Wembley

arch. A metallic voice rang out into the
stunned silence.

'People of Earth, go to your homes and
stay there. This is an order. Failure to obey
will be punishable by death. This planet is
now a province of the Zargon Empire.'

One

Wanted –
Dead or Alive

'Charlotte, get away from that window! They'll see you!'

Olivia grabbed Charlotte's T-shirt and pulled her down onto the floor.

Outside a hover car moved slowly along the street. An amplified voice boomed from a loudspeaker mounted on the back, telling everyone who had a musical instrument to take it to the nearest MIB 'harmony' camp, where it would be 'sanitised'. The voice was as cold as an arctic winter and it was clear that when it said 'sanitised' it meant destroyed.

Charlotte smoothed down her T-shirt and frowned at Olivia. 'Yeah, all right, Liv,' she said. 'I was just trying to get a sneaky look at the creepoids.' She glanced at the other girls sitting huddled together in the room. Fear radiated from them.

'Well, don't!' snapped Kelly. ''Cos if you see them, then there's a good chance they'll see you.'

Charlotte pouted and looked sulky. 'Hey, I know they're aliens, Kelly, but I don't think they've got X-ray vision.'

Kelly sighed. 'Well, let's hope not, 'cos if they do they'll be able to see right through the walls of this house – and then we're dead!'

A girl with wild hair shook her head. 'Well, not *dead* exactly, but mind-wiped.'

'That's right, Eve,' said Yaz. 'And that's worse.'

'Er, excuse me,' said Charlotte, 'but how come being mind-wiped is worse than being dead?'

'Because when you're mind-wiped you forget how to sing,' replied Yaz. 'And I'd rather be dead than live in a world without music.'

'Don't worry, Yaz,' said Liv. 'That isn't going to happen. MIB aren't going to catch us and take us to the 'harmony' camps.'

Kelly snorted. 'You hope!' She pulled out a phone from her pocket. 'Every time I check the net it's full of stuff about musicians being carted off to the camps.'

She stared at the screen and groaned. The other girls knew more bad news was coming.

'And, get this. MIB is offering a huge reward for our capture. They want us dead or alive!'

TWO

On the Run

Eve grabbed Kelly's phone and stared at the screen. 'It's true,' she groaned. 'The Zargons are saying they'll pay ten million pounds for information that leads to our capture!'

'Wow,' said Liv. 'That's serious money.'

'It is,' said Yaz. 'But no way is any human going to grass us up to a bunch of alien music-haters.'

Kelly grimaced. 'Don't be so sure,' she said. 'Some people would sell their grannies for the price of a song download – let alone ten million quid!'

At that moment Finn, the band's roadie, strode into the room. His face was strained and pale and he looked like he hadn't slept for a week.

'OK, girls,' he said gruffly. 'It's time we hit the road. MIB agents are all over this city like a rash, so I need to take you somewhere where nobody knows you.'

Eve raised her eyebrows sceptically. 'Hey, there isn't any such place.'

Finn grinned at her. 'Oh yes there is. It's an abandoned village deep in the countryside.

Nobody has lived there for years. It's kind of like a ghost town.'

Liv's eyes lit up. 'Wow, that sounds cool! Is it really haunted?'

'Don't be such a dummy, Liv,' said Charlotte. 'Ghosts don't actually exist.'

Liv shrugged. 'Yeah, well nobody believed aliens were real either, until the Zargons invaded.'

'That's true,' said Kelly. She looked at Finn. 'So what's the story? Is it haunted?'

Finn shook his head. 'No, the villagers all moved out sometime in the last century when the army wanted to use the place for training elite soldiers. By the time the special forces had finished with it the villagers were all too old to move back. So now it's empty.'

'All right,' said Eve. 'But how come you know about it?'

'Because I lived in that part of the world when I was a boy. Me and my mates were always daring each other to spend the night in that village – but we never did. It's way too spooky.'

Finn ran his hands through his spiky hair. 'Believe me girls, nobody ever goes there.'

Yaz clapped her hands in delight. 'Hey, it sounds like the perfect place for us to hide out.'

'Well, if we're going we'd better be quick.' Charlotte was looking out of the window again. "Cos an MIB snatch squad has just pulled up outside the front door!'

Three

The Ghost Village

The girls and Finn hurtled down the stairs and out of the back door, just as the snatch squad smashed their way into the house. They raced across the back garden and clambered over the fence, dropping down into the quiet street.

Finn ran over to a battered old van. He wrenched the cab door open and leapt inside.

'Get in the back,' he yelled at the girls. 'We don't have much time.'

For a split second the girls stood there open-mouthed. They were used to travelling in stretch limos – not beaten-up old bangers. Then they heard shouts coming from behind the fence, so they piled into the van and slammed the doors. Finn rammed his foot down hard on the accelerator and, with a squeal of tyres and a smell of burning rubber, the van roared away.

* * * * * * *

Several hours later, Finn drove into the abandoned village and pulled up outside the school. The girls tumbled out of the van and stretched their tired and aching bodies.

'That wreck is a total bone-shaker,' grumbled Charlotte.

'Yeah,' agreed Eve. 'It has got to be the world's most uncomfortable van.'

'Oh stop moaning,' said Yaz. 'We made it here in one piece and that's the main thing!'

Kelly nodded. 'That's right.' She turned to Finn. 'And thanks for risking everything to get us here.'

Finn smiled. 'Hey, no worries. I'm just doing my job. I *am* your road manager, after all.'

Kelly looked around at the deserted village. The houses were dark and sinister and cast eerie shadows everywhere. 'And this is where the road has brought us. It's not exactly Hollywood, is it?'

Liv shuddered. 'No, it isn't. But it could be a movie set for a horror movie.'

Eve nodded. 'Yes, one of those horror movies where a bunch of teenage girls get murdered by an evil maniac.'

The girls gulped and all moved closer together. 'Well, we'd better not split up then,' said Yaz. 'There's safety in numbers.'

Finn smiled. His teeth flashed white in the moonlight. 'Go into the school and try to make yourselves comfortable, while I

find somewhere to hide the van,' he said.
'And try not to eat all the chocolate, crisps
and biscuits I bought at the service station
before I get back!'

The girls watched him drive off. Then
they crept nervously into the old school
building.

Four
Missing

The five girls made their way into the
school hall. Moonlight streamed in through
the windows. There was a stage at one end
and an old upright piano stood against the
wall. They jumped up onto the stage and
put their provisions down next to them.

'We won't eat anything until Finn gets
back,' said Kelly.

The other girls agreed that was only fair.

'Though I guess he wouldn't mind if we just nibbled a sandwich while we waited for him,' said Liv.

'Of course he wouldn't,' said Eve, as she ripped the wrapping from a sandwich and crammed it into her mouth.

That did it. All the girls grabbed at the food and it wasn't long before they had eaten everything Finn had bought.

'You guys are just so greedy,' said Kelly, when the feeding frenzy was over.

'Yeah, well I didn't notice you holding back,' retorted Charlotte. 'I thought you were a magician 'cos you were making chocolate bars disappear like magic.'

Kelly scowled and folded her arms. If Charlotte wanted a fight, then Kelly was more than ready to oblige. Charlotte scowled back at her, but before either of them could say anything, Yaz spoke up.

'Hey, where's Finn? He's been gone for hours.'

Eve bit her bottom lip. Suddenly she had a bad feeling about this. 'Yes, where is he?' she said. 'He can't still be hiding the van.'

Then the door to the school hall crashed open and an MIB snatch squad strutted in. They held Finn captive.

'No, he isn't hiding the van,' snarled the MIB captain. 'He's right here with us!'

Five

The Fat Lady Sings

The MIB agents pushed Finn to the floor. 'I'm sorry, girls,' he said. 'They grabbed me as I was on my way back here.'

'But how did they know this is where we were?' asked Eve. 'We gave them the slip back at the house.'

The alien captain made a barking sound. The girls realised he was laughing, and the sound of it chilled their blood.

'We have been keeping an eye on your road manager. We guessed he knew where you were hiding. So, when he bought an old van, an MIB agent planted a bug in it. Then, when you 'gave us the slip' in London, all we had to do was activate it and follow you.' His eyes glowed a curious yellow colour in the dim light. 'Now we will take you to the nearest 'harmony' camp. It is time you girls had your minds wiped!'

The MIB snatch squad advanced menacingly towards the girls.

'Just wait up,' said Kelly. 'I know you guys can't wait to silence us forever but, as my mum says, it ain't over until the fat lady sings.'

The MIB captain looked puzzled. 'Who is this fat lady?' he hissed. 'We will find her and wipe her mind too.'

'Good luck with that,' laughed Yaz. Then she did a somersault from the stage and landed, nimble as a cat, right next to the piano.

Before the startled MIB agents could stop her, she began to play. The aliens covered their ears with their hands.

'No, stop!' they screamed.

Yaz looked up at the others. 'Hit it, girls,' she yelled. 'These guys want harmonies, so let's give it to them!'

Immediately, the girls launched into their trademark five-part harmonies. The sound rang out pure and clear as a mountain stream. The MIB agents stumbled and staggered like marionettes with their strings cut. Then cracks like those in shattered glass appeared on their faces. As the girls sang, the alien's skin began to bubble and dissolve. Then, as the song soared to a climax, the aliens melted into a jelly-like sludge before the girls' eyes.

'Come on, girls,' yelled Finn. 'There's no time for an encore. We need to be long gone

before the next MIB squad comes looking for us.'

The girls leapt down from the stage. 'Where are we going?' asked Eve.

'I don't know,' he replied. 'But one thing's for sure. It won't be to a mind-wipe camp!'

Will the Zargons ever defeat **GirlFriendZ** ?

What do you think?